She's Brown Like Me!

by Febrah Hall

Printed in the United States of America by
T&J Publishers (Atlanta, GA.)
www.TandJPublishers.com

Illustrations and Cover Design by Nikembe Pierce
Book Format and Layout by Timothy Flemming, Jr. (T&J Publishers)

ISBN: 978-1-7360003-9-7

To contact author, go to:

FChisholm87@gmail.com
Facebook: Febrah Hall Author
Instagram: FebrahHallTheAuthor

I would like to dedicate this book to my husband for encour-
aging and motivating me to always keep going; my two sons;
and any student that may have been inspired by having me as
a "brown" teacher.

Zhara's family was moving to the next town yet again. Zhara's father is in the military so they moved very often. Even though she was used to moving, it didn't make it any easier each time.

   While in the car she couldn't stop thinking about all the great times she had with all of her friends she made while at her last school; playing tag, swinging on the swings at recess, dancing her heart out at the after school dances! She couldn't help but feel that her world was over.

   "Zhara!" her little brother Zane exclaimed, as he continued to tap her on the shoulder. "Come on, you've got to snap out of it. We're almost at the new house... I bet it's big, what do you think?!" Zhara had no response, she just continued to just mope looking out the car window.

Still in a sour mood, Zhara prepared for her first day at her new school moving as slow as a slug. "Are you trying to make us late on purpose?" Her mom yelled from the kitchen. "Let's go, let's go!"

Zhara's mom had a good talk with her on the ride to school to try and lift up her spirits. It helped some, but not enough. When she arrived at school everything was already different from the time she stepped in the door.

Thinking to herself: "at my last school we sat in the hallway outside of our room. Here we've got to all sit in the cafeteria. All these people are staring at me!" This increased Zhara's anxiety, and her mom's talk now had no

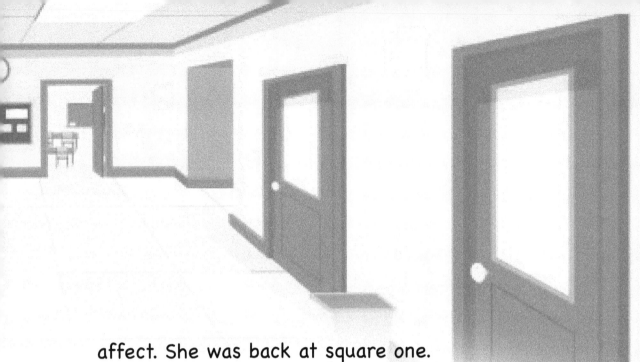

affect. She was back at square one.

"Fifth graders, please line up quietly according to your homeroom teacher." Zhara recognizes her teacher's last name and heads toward the line. Once she arrives in class she overhears other students talking saying "This lady Isn't Mrs. Sammuels. What's up with that?" Zhara's family wasn't in town early enough for Meet the Teacher, so she had no idea what her teacher would look like. The woman in the class explained that Mrs. Sammuels had a last minute emergency this morning so she was the substitute for today; but that Mrs. Sammuels should be here tomorrow.

Zhara sees her brother at dismissal and is so relieved to see a familiar face. "Hey, how did it go?" Zane asks cheerfully. "How do you think it went? It was terrible! Everything is so different here, and I didn't even get to meet my teacher to know if I'd like her or not. This sucks, I really wish we were back at our old school."

Neither Zane, nor their mom and dad were able to cheer Zhara up that night. "She seems so defeated. I'm starting to really worry about her." Zhara's mom explained to her dad as they talked privately in the kitchen. "It's only been one day of school, she will begin to love it here just like you and I have... Give it time." Dad replied.

The next morning comes and Zhara is unhappy again about going to the new school with all the new changes and people. Her brother Zane gives her a slight tap on the shoulder and smiles. Signaling to her that it's going to get better and to cheer up.

Zhara begins her day again in the cafeteria with all the students. The teacher on duty informs the students it is time to line up and go to their homeroom. As Zhara is approaching her teacher's class she notices that her actual teacher is here today which was exciting; but not only that, her teacher is African American. Zhara is in complete shock! From Kindergarten all the way through 4th grade she had never experienced having a Black teacher. Zhara's shock grew into excitement and joy.

Mrs. Sammuels talks to Zhara at the door and introduces herself. Zhara being as excited as she was couldn't help but to blurt out her thoughts. "You're brown like me! I've never had an African American teacher before." Hearing this brings the biggest smile across Mrs. Sammuels face! This brings about an instant connection because the teacher then begins to think about her first time having an African American teacher too!

Zhara is so excited at carline; she can hardly wait for her father to come pick her up so she can tell him all about her day! "Zhara Hale, Zhara Hale...pole 2" Zhara leaped up from her seat and walked as quickly as she could to get outside to her father's car. "Hey Daddy!" she yelled as soon as she opened the door. Her father was quite shocked by her greeting since the last few days she had been very sad and not very cheerful at all. "Well hello buttercup! So happy to see a smile on that beautiful face! I'm going to assume that you had a much better day at school today?" Dad asked. "It was awesome! We learned about the scientific method, place value, and some other stuff too. But Dad, the BEST part of the day you'll never guess! So on yesterday, I had a sub but today I got to meet my teacher, and she's African American!" she replied. Zane interjected "Really? That's pretty cool.".

Zhara continued to talk with her dad about her great day all the way home from school. Zane and her dad both were so thrilled to see her happy that they just continued to listen and didn't say a word. Over dinner she was still talking about it. Even to the point that she was cutting off her brother. Her parents eventually had to get Zhara to calm her excitement so that everyone would have a chance to talk about their day. After dinner she video called her good friend from her last school to share the news with her too!

The next morning Zhara has a much better attitude and is much less reluctant about going to school.

During school she realizes that not only is Mrs. Sammuels cool because she's African American; she's also funny, hip, and a great teacher! She helped Zhara enjoy learning more than any other teacher ever had before. As the school year continued she began making new friends, gaining more confidence in her academics and herself in general.

By the end of the school year Mrs. Sammuels had become Zhara's overall favorite teacher. She absolutely hated that she was having to move on to middle school. Each year during Teacher Appreciation Week Zhara would send Mrs. Sammuels a letter thanking her and sharing what was new in her life. She updated her about joining the cheerleading team, the Journalism staff, the basketball team, and the Drama Club.

Unfortunately, Zhara's family had to move once more. Though she wasn't thrilled about moving, she definitely adjusted better than she did the last go round. All the way up into 12th grade Zhara continued to communicate with her favorite teacher, and often. Zhara's senior year Mrs. Sammuels came to see her graduate high school; even though the drive was hours away! Zhara continued to do well in her academics and became the salutatorian of her graduating class. In her graduation speech, she mentioned Mrs. Sammuels and how she felt that having her as a teacher made a major impact on her future. Mrs. Sammuels listened to Zhara's speech with such pride, her heart was full.

Zhara invited Mrs. Sammuels, but had no idea that she was actually in attendance at her graduation. She was ecstatic to see Mrs. Sammuels standing with her parents after the ceremony. "No way... Mrs. Sammuels?!"

she asked, as she walked towards her family. "Yes ma'am, you guessed it. It's me!" Mrs. Sammuels replied. They greeted each other with open arms. After Zhara spoke with her family and friends, she quickly reunited with her former teacher, caught up on missed events and more. Zhara expressed to Mrs. Sammuels that she was going to college majoring in English, and her long-term goal was to become an author. "I'm planning to start on my first book this summer. It is actually inspired by you!" Zhara says. Mrs. Sammuels looks pretty shocked. "Meeting you was a major turning point for me. I never had a teacher to understand the things I truly experienced, you were so relatable. You helped me love school. Having a Black teacher made a world of difference. So I'm going to name my book 'She's brown like me'."

About The Author

Febrah Hall was born on September 12, 1987, in Tuskegee, Alabama. After highschool, she got her Bachelor's Degree from Troy University in Elementary Education, and after that received her Masters of Education from Auburn University at Montgomery in School Counseling. She is currently an elementary teacher and has been for the last ten years. "She's Brown like me" is her very first book.

To contact the author, go to:

FChisholm87@gmail.com
Facebook: Febrah Hall Author
Instagram: FebrahHallTheAuthor

CPSIA information can be obtained
at www.ICGtesting.com
Printed in the USA
BVHW022314130421
604820BV00010B/908